Usborne English Readers

Level 3

The Wizard of Oz

Retold by Mairi Mackinnon

Illustrated by Davide Ortu

English language consultant: Peter Viney

Contents

3

The Wizard of Oz

40

About the story

41

Activities

46

Word list

You can listen to the story online here:
www.usborneenglishreaders.com/
wizardofoz

Dorothy lived with her Uncle Henry and her Aunt Em in a small wooden farmhouse. From the house, Dorothy couldn't see another house, or a hill, or a tree, but only the prairie, the wide open grassland in the middle of America.

Uncle Henry was a farmer. He worked all day, and he hardly ever spoke.

Aunt Em was his wife. She worked hard, too, and she hardly ever smiled.

One thing made Dorothy smile, and that was Toto, her little black dog. Toto played with Dorothy and made her laugh, and she loved him.

Today, though, Toto didn't want to play. The sky was dark, the wind was wild and he was hiding under the bed.

"There's a tornado coming," said Uncle Henry. "I'm going to see that the animals are safe. Em, Dorothy, get down to the cellar." The cellar was a place under the house where they could be safe from tornadoes. Those terrible prairie storms could smash a house to pieces.

Aunt Em climbed down, and Dorothy had just caught Toto when the house shook and she fell on the floor. Then the wind lifted the whole house into the air.

Dorothy was very frightened, but the house stayed up in the air. It was moving quite gently, like a boat. Dorothy lay down on her little bed, and Toto lay down beside her. Soon they were asleep.

There was a bump, and Dorothy woke up. The house was on the ground, and there was bright sunlight outside. Dorothy looked out and saw a beautiful country of green grass and fruit trees. Then she saw four strange people. There were three little men, wearing blue clothes and boots and pointed hats, and one woman wearing a white dress and white hat.

"Welcome, Great Witch," said the woman. "Thank you for killing the Wicked Witch of the East."

"But I'm not a witch," said Dorothy. "I've never killed anyone."

"Your house did," said the woman. She pointed to two legs under the house. They were wearing silver shoes. Suddenly the legs disappeared in a puff of smoke.

"Oh no!" said Dorothy.

"Don't worry," said the woman. "She was very wicked. She made these people her slaves. Now she is dead, and they are free. You should have the silver shoes. I know that they are magic, but I don't know how they work."

"Witches? Magic?" asked Dorothy. "Where am I? And when can I go back home? Uncle Henry and Aunt Em must be worried about me."

"You are in the Land of Oz," said the woman. "I am the Good Witch of the North. I'd like to help you, but I'm not sure how. I think you should go to the Emerald City and ask the Great Wizard. It's a long way, but it's easy to find. Just follow the road made of yellow bricks. Goodbye, my dear, and good luck." The three men bowed, and the Good Witch turned around three times and disappeared in another puff of smoke.

Dorothy looked at her old shoes. "I can't walk far in these," she said. She tried the silver slippers, and they fitted perfectly. They were surprisingly comfortable, too. Then she ate some breakfast, and went with Toto to find the yellow brick road. They soon saw it, leading away over the hills, and they started walking.

After a few hours, they stopped to rest beside a field. Dorothy saw a scarecrow wearing old blue clothes and a blue hat, just like the little people she had met earlier.

"Good morning," said the scarecrow.

Dorothy was very surprised, but she answered politely. "Good morning. How are you?"

"Hmm," said the scarecrow. "I'm rather bored. I'd really like to get down from this wooden pole and leave this field. Perhaps you can help me?" Dorothy lifted him up and put him on the ground. "Oh, thank you. That's better." He shook his arms and legs. "Now, where are we going?"

"I'm going to the Emerald City," said Dorothy. "Do you know it?"

"I don't know anything," said the scarecrow sadly. "I have no brains."

"Perhaps the Great Wizard can give you brains," said Dorothy. "When we find him, we can ask."

"Do you think so?" The scarecrow looked pleased. They walked further along the road and into a forest. The road was rougher here, and it was dark under the trees. At last they saw a wooden house.

"I think we should stay here tonight," said Dorothy. Inside the house she found some dry leaves in one corner, and she lay down to sleep.

The next morning, Dorothy heard a strange sound. "There's someone outside," she said. "I think he's hurt." Near the house she saw a man made of tin, standing quite still.

"Did you make that noise?" she asked.

"Help me!" said the tin man. "I've been outside in the rain, and now I can't move."

"What can I do?" asked Dorothy.

"Find some oil," said the tin man. Dorothy found an oilcan by the house, and poured oil over his neck and his arms and his legs.

The tin man started moving. "Oh, thank you!" he said. "Where are you going? May I travel with you?"

"Certainly," said Dorothy. "We're going to the Emerald City, to see the Great Wizard."

"He's going to give me some brains!" said the scarecrow.

"Really?" said the tin man. "Do you think he could give me a heart? I used to have one, and I miss it."

"Let's ask him," said Dorothy.

They walked through the forest. Sometimes Dorothy heard animal noises among the trees. She was glad that the scarecrow and the tin man were with her. Toto walked close beside her now.

Suddenly they heard a roar, and an enormous lion jumped on to the road. He knocked the scarecrow to the roadside. The lion tried to attack the tin man, too, but his metal body was too hard. Toto ran forward, barking, and the lion opened his mouth wide...

Dorothy ran forward and hit him on the nose. "Don't you dare!" she shouted. "He's only a little dog. You're a big coward!"

The lion looked sad. "It's true," he said. "Everyone thinks I'm brave, but I never hurt anybody. Whenever I roar, they all run away. I would like to be brave."

"Perhaps you could ask the Great Wizard to help," said the tin man.

"I'm sure he could," said the scarecrow. "Come with us."

At last the road left the forest. Now they could see fields of flowers all around them, bright red poppies. "They're beautiful," said Dorothy, "and they smell wonderful." She sat down and closed her eyes. Toto lay down beside her, and the lion yawned.

"Something's wrong," said the scarecrow. "The poppies are making them sleep!"

"But you're all right," said the tin man, "and so am I, because we can't smell anything. Let's carry Dorothy and Toto to somewhere safe. Lion, you must run as fast as you can, before you fall asleep too."

They carried Dorothy and Toto far away from the poppy fields. Soon the lion felt more awake, and much better.

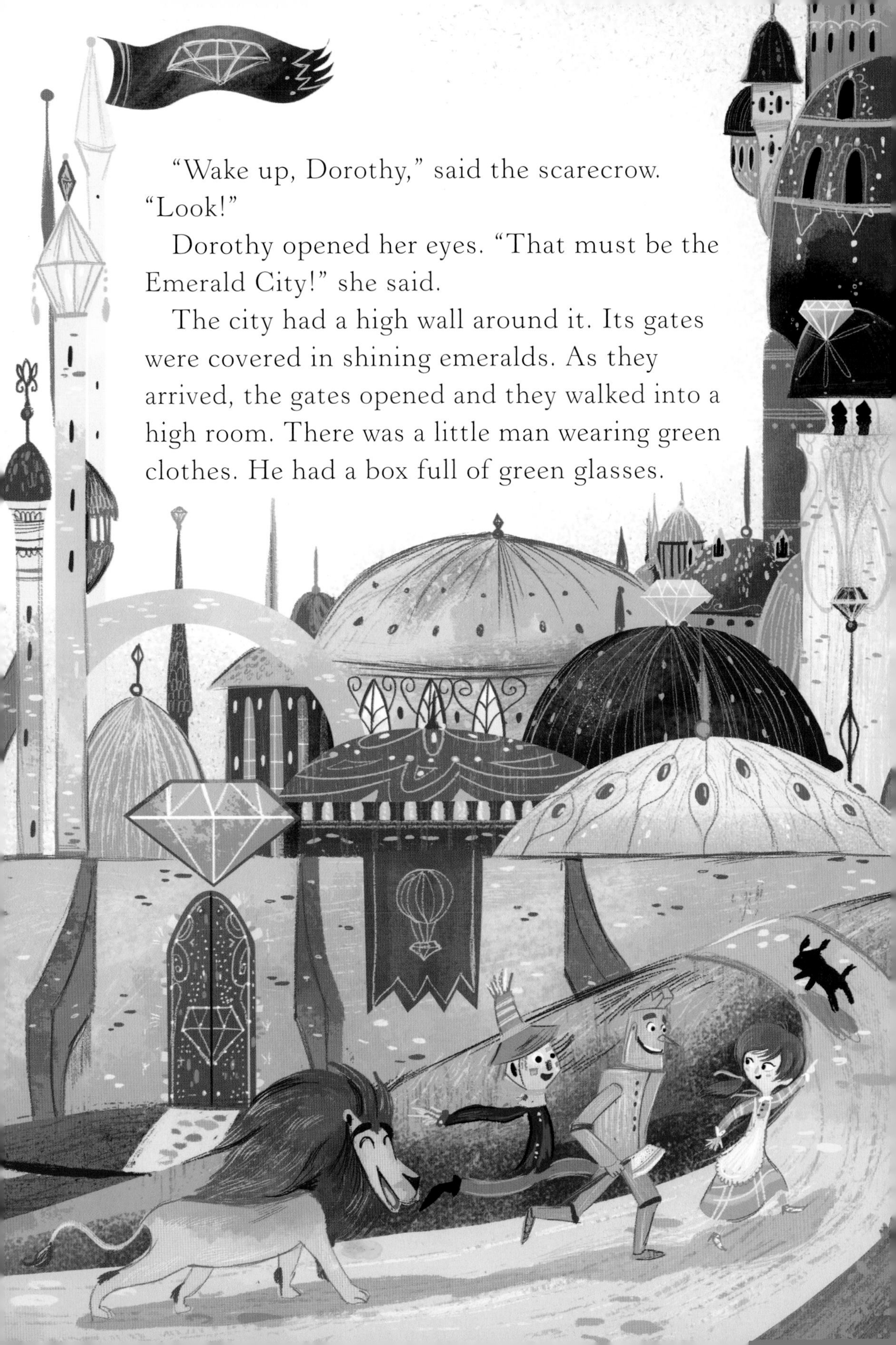

"Wake up, Dorothy," said the scarecrow. "Look!"

Dorothy opened her eyes. "That must be the Emerald City!" she said.

The city had a high wall around it. Its gates were covered in shining emeralds. As they arrived, the gates opened and they walked into a high room. There was a little man wearing green clothes. He had a box full of green glasses.

“Welcome to our city,” he said. “You must wear these glasses, or the emerald light will hurt your eyes.” Even Toto had to wear some. “What would you like to do now?” the man asked.

“We’ve come to see the Great Wizard,” said Dorothy.

The little man was so surprised that he almost fell over. “That’s impossible!” he said. “The Great Wizard never sees strangers. I’ve never seen him myself. I’ve only heard his voice.”

"Please ask him," said Dorothy. "It's important." The friends followed the little man through the city. They saw green everywhere: grand green houses, green trees and green flowers. Green people walked in the green streets under a green sky. Dorothy thought they looked happy.

They reached an enormous palace, and the little man went inside. Finally he came back.

"You're very lucky. The Great Wizard will see you," he said. "You must go in one at a time."

Dorothy picked up Toto, and went into a huge hall. At one end was a throne, and on the throne was a giant green head without a body.

"I am the Great Wizard," said the head. It had quite a normal voice. "What do you want from me?"

"Please," said Dorothy, "I want to go home to Uncle Henry and Aunt Em. What shall I do?"

"You must kill the Wicked Witch of the West," said the head.

"I can't do that!" said Dorothy.

"It's the only way," said the head. "Now go!"

Dorothy came out and told her friends. They felt very sorry for her, but they couldn't think how to help. "It's your turn now, Scarecrow" said Dorothy.

On the throne was a beautiful lady with an emerald crown.

"I am the Great Wizard," said the lady. "What do you want from me?"

"I... I would like some brains," said the scarecrow.

"Well, then, you must kill the Wicked Witch of the West," said the lady.

"But that's what you told Dorothy!"

"I don't mind who kills her," said the lady, "but until she is dead, I can't help you."

The scarecrow went out and told his friends.

"That's rather cruel," said the tin man. "Perhaps the wizard doesn't have a heart, either." He went into the hall next. He saw a monster on the throne, with five eyes and five arms and five legs.

"I am the Great Wizard," said the monster. "What do you want from me?"

"I'd like a loving heart," said the tin man.

"Well, then, you must help Dorothy and the scarecrow to kill the Wicked Witch of the West," said the monster.

Finally it was the lion's turn. "I'm not afraid of monsters," he said; but instead of a monster, he saw a ball of green fire. "You want me to make you brave?" asked a voice from the fire. "Then first you must kill the Wicked Witch of the West."

Slowly, the four friends left the palace. "What shall we do now?" asked Dorothy.

"I suppose we should try to find the witch, at least," said the scarecrow. They went back to the city gates, and the little man took their green glasses.

"Which road will take us to the Wicked Witch of the West?" asked Dorothy.

"There is no road," said the man. "Walk towards the evening sun. She'll know that you are coming."

The friends walked through fields of soft grass, then over hills where the grass was rougher. There were no trees now, and no farms or houses. At night, Dorothy and Toto and the lion lay down on the grass to sleep, and the scarecrow and the tin man watched.

Someone else was watching, too. The Wicked Witch of the West only had one eye, but she could see a long way with that eye. She was angry to find strangers in her country.

"Slaves!" she shouted. Some strange little people came in, wearing yellow clothes. "Slaves, go and fight them!"

The little people took sharp spears, and ran to meet Dorothy and her friends. First the scarecrow and the tin man stood in front of the others. The little people threw their spears, but they couldn't hurt them. Then the lion roared, and the little people ran away.

"Fools!" said the witch. She put on a golden cap, and said a magic spell. A crowd of flying monkeys filled the air.

"Bring me the four strangers," said the witch. "Wait, I don't need the scarecrow and the tin man. Just bring me the lion and the little girl."

The monkeys flew out, picked up the four friends and flew back towards the witch's castle. They brought Dorothy and the lion, but they dropped the tin man on the rocky ground, and threw the scarecrow into a tall tree.

When the witch saw Dorothy's silver shoes, she smiled. "She doesn't know what those shoes can do," she thought.

"You, girl, you can work for me," she said. "Fill that bucket, and start washing the floor. Lion, you can pull my carriage when I go out."

"I'm not a horse," said the lion. "I will never pull your carriage."

"You'll have no food until you do," said the witch. "Do you want to die, like your friends?"

"You're horrible!" said Dorothy. She threw a bucket of water at the witch.

"Help!" screamed the witch. "Stupid girl! Water is the worst thing for me! I'm melting!" She became smaller and smaller, until only her clothes and the golden cap were left in a pool of water.

"You've killed her!" the little people cheered. "We're free, we're free!"

"I'm glad about that," said Dorothy. "I just wish the scarecrow and the tin man could be here."

"Can we help?" asked the little people. They fetched the broken pieces of the tin man, and carefully repaired him. Then they cut down the tree where the scarecrow had fallen, and lifted him out. The four friends were together again.

"Now we must go back to the Emerald City, and ask the wizard to help us," said Dorothy. "But how can we find it from here?"

"Try using the golden cap," said the little people. "Read the spell inside it, and the monkeys will do whatever you want. The magic will work three times."

Dorothy said the spell, then asked the flying monkeys to carry them. The scarecrow and the tin man were a little nervous, but the monkeys held them carefully all the way.

The little man at the gate was surprised to see them. "You were supposed to kill the witch!" he said.

"We did," said Dorothy. "We melted her. So now we really have to see the wizard."

They went straight to the palace and into the green hall, but there was nobody on the throne.

"Where is the wizard?" asked Dorothy.

"I am the Great Wizard," said a voice high above them. "What do you want from me?"

"We did what you asked," said Dorothy. "Now you have to keep your promises."

"Oh," said the voice. "I don't think I can."

The lion roared angrily. Toto was so surprised that he jumped and knocked over a wooden screen in the corner. He was even more surprised to see an old man behind the screen.

"Who are you?" asked the tin man.

"I am the Great Wizard," the old man said in a normal voice.

"But what about the giant head..?" said Dorothy.

"The beautiful lady..?" said the scarecrow.

"The monster..?"

"The ball of fire..?"

"They were all tricks," said the old man. He took them to a small room and showed them some shapes made of paper and cloth. "I pull ropes to make them move. And I can change my voice, so that it seems to come from somewhere else."

"You're not a wizard at all?" asked Dorothy.

“Oh no, my dear, I’m a balloonist. One day I was in my balloon, and the ropes got stuck so I couldn’t let the hot air out. I floated in the sky for two days, until I came down in this strange country. Everyone thought I was a wizard because I had come from the sky. They built this city for me, and I made them wear green glasses so that it looked more interesting.

Then I heard about the four witches. I didn’t mind the good witches, but I was afraid of the two wicked ones. When I heard that you had killed the Wicked Witch of the East, I decided to send you to the other one. I promised you anything you wanted, but I can’t do anything about it now.”

"Then you're a very bad man," said Dorothy.

"Oh no," said the balloonist. "I'm a good man, but I'm afraid I'm a very bad wizard."

"So you can't give me brains?" asked the scarecrow.

"Or a heart?" asked the tin man.

"Or make me brave?" asked the lion.

"I think you are wise and kind and brave already," said the balloonist. "But if you like..."

He took a box of pins, and made a little space in the top of the scarecrow's head. Then he dropped the pins in, closed the top of the head and put the scarecrow's hat back on. "How do you feel now?" he asked.

"Very wise indeed!" said the scarecrow. "Thank you!"

The balloonist picked up a small heart-shaped cushion. "This is for you," he told the tin man. "May I cut a hole in your body? It won't hurt." He cut a small hole, put the cushion inside and closed the hole again. "How do you feel now?" he asked.

"I feel… so many things I never felt before!" said the tin man. "Thank you!"

The balloonist took a small bottle and gave it to the lion. "Drink this," he said.

"Ah, it tastes like fire!" said the lion. "I feel brave enough for anything! Thank you!"

The balloonist turned to Dorothy. “For you, I have an idea,” he said. “I’m tired of tricks, and I‘d like to go home, too. We’ll make another balloon. We’ll float away from Oz and go back to the prairie.”

Dorothy and her friends helped to put the balloon together, and at last it was ready to fly. A huge crowd came to say goodbye to them. Dorothy hugged her friends, picked up Toto and climbed into the balloon basket.

Suddenly Toto saw a cat in the crowd, and he jumped out. "Come back, come back!" shouted Dorothy, but Toto was busy chasing the cat. Dorothy climbed out of the basket, and it lifted into the air.

"Stop!" she said.

"I'm sorry!" shouted the balloonist. "I can't!" The balloon lifted higher and higher. "Goodbye, my dear."

Dorothy sat down and cried. "How can I go home now?" The tin man put his arm around her and cried a little, too.

"Why don't you ask the flying monkeys?" said the scarecrow, using his new brains.

"That's a good idea!" said Dorothy. She put on the golden cap and said the spell, but the monkeys shook their heads. "We can't leave this country," they said. "Remember, you can only use the spell once more."

"Doesn't anybody know?" asked Dorothy. Then she saw the little man from the city gate.

"You could ask the Good Witch of the South," he said. "She's the most powerful witch of all."

"We'll come with you," said the lion, the tin man and the scarecrow. So Dorothy put the golden cap on her head, and asked the monkeys to carry them to the Good Witch's castle.

The witch had a long white dress, and beautiful red hair and blue eyes. She smiled at the four friends. "What can I do for you?"

"Please," whispered Dorothy. "Help me to go home."

"I think I can do that," said the witch. "Will you give me the golden cap? You won't need it now, but I can use it." Then she turned to the scarecrow. "What will you do when Dorothy has gone?"

The scarecrow smiled shyly. "The people of the Emerald City have asked me to be their king," he said.

"And a very wise king you will be," said the witch. "I shall ask the monkeys to take you back there."

She turned to the tin man. "And what will you do?"

The tin man smiled, too. "I'd like to go back to the little people of the west, who repaired me so well," he said.

"They will be good friends to you," said the witch. "I shall ask the monkeys to take you. And you, Lion?"

"I'd like to go back to the forest, to be King of the Animals," said the lion.

"You'll be the bravest king they've ever had," said the witch. "I shall ask the monkeys one last time."

"Now, Dorothy, just tap your silver shoes together three times, and tell them where you want to go."

"Oh!" said Dorothy. "Why didn't I try that at the beginning?"

"But then I would still be in a field, with no brains," said the scarecrow.

"And I would be stuck in a forest, with no heart," said the tin man.

"And I wouldn't be brave, and I wouldn't be King of the Animals," said the lion.

"That's true," said Dorothy. "I'm glad that you all have what you wanted, and I'm glad that you have been my friends. I'll miss you!" She hugged them all, and thanked the good witch. Then she picked up Toto, closed her eyes, tapped the shoes together and said, "Take me home to Aunt Em!"

She fell with a bump on the long grass of the prairie. She could see a new wooden farmhouse, and beside it was someone who she knew very well.

"Aunt Em!" cried Dorothy, running towards her.

Aunt Em put her arms around her. "Dear child, where in the world have you been?"

"In the Land of Oz," said Dorothy. "And so has Toto. But oh, Aunt Em, there's no place like home!"

About the story

L. Frank Baum was born in America in 1856. He had lots of different jobs during his life, including actor, shopkeeper, newspaper reporter and salesman, but he always loved to tell stories.

In 1900, he wrote *The Wonderful Wizard of Oz*, the story of a girl called Dorothy and her adventures in the magical Land of Oz. The book was a huge success. American children were used to reading fairy tales from Europe. They enjoyed reading about a girl from an ordinary American home instead.

In 1939, Baum's story was made into a film. The actress Judy Garland played Dorothy. In the film, the magic shoes are red instead of silver, because it was hard to see silver ones on the yellow brick road.

Baum wrote thirteen more books about Dorothy and the Land of Oz. They sold millions of copies in over 50 languages.

Activities

The answers are on page 48.

What are they? What can they do?

Match the descriptions to the pictures below.
Each description has two parts.

1. 

2. 

3. 

4.

5.  

A. The golden cap...
B. The silver shoes...
C. The bucket of water...
D. The heart-shaped cushion...
E. The small bottle...

a. ...will make you brave.
b. ...will give you feelings.
c. ...will take you home.
d. ...will melt a wicked witch.
e. ...will bring the flying monkeys to help you.

Missing words

Choose a word from the list at the bottom of the page to finish each sentence.

home	monster	water	strangers
away	tricks	poppies	farm
brain	city	heart	coward

Mixed-up story

Can you put these pictures and sentences in order?

A.

"There's no place like home!" said Dorothy.

B.

She threw a bucket of water at the witch.

C.

The gates were covered in shining emeralds.

D.

The balloon lifted higher and higher...

E.

"You must kill the Wicked Witch of the West," said the head.

F.

Dorothy went with Toto to find the yellow brick road.

G.

"You should have the silver shoes," said the woman.

H.

Toto was surprised to see an old man.

I.

The wind lifted the whole house into the air.

I want...

What does each character want? Choose the right sentence.

Who's who?

Can you match the characters to the sentences on the right?

1.Toto

2. Aunt Em and Uncle Henry

3. The Good Witch of the South

4. The Wizard of Oz

5. The Wicked Witch of the West

6. The Good Witch of the North

A. She tells Dorothy how the shoes work.

B. He likes chasing cats.

C. They built a new farmhouse.

D. She wants the lion to pull her carriage.

E. He's really a balloonist.

F. She thinks Dorothy is a witch.

Word list

balloon (n)

balloonist (n) the person who flies a balloon.

basket (n)

bark (v) when a dog barks, it makes a loud noise to show that it is excited or angry.

bow (v) to show respect for someone by bending forward.

brain, brains (n) the thing inside your head that makes you intelligent.

brick (n) something that you use to build walls and houses.

bump (n) when something hits something else suddenly and hard.

bucket (n) something that you use to carry water or other liquids.

cap (n) a type of hat.

carriage (n) something that you ride in, usually pulled by horses.

cellar (n) a room underground.

cheer (v) when you cheer, you shout to show that you're happy or to encourage people.

coward (n) someone who isn't brave and doesn't want to fight.

cushion (n) something soft that you put on a chair to make yourself comfortable.

emerald (n) a precious green stone.

hug (n) a way of showing someone that you love them by putting your arms around them and holding them close.

hardly ever (adv) almost never.

lift (v) to pick something or someone up and carry them through the air.

melt (v) when something solid turns to liquid, like ice to water.

oilcan (n) a container for machine oil.

pin (n) something that you use to hold pieces of cloth together.

pole (n) a long, thin wooden stick.

poppy (n) a wild flower, usually red.

pour (v) when you pour something (usually something wet, like water), you drop it over something else or into something else.

prairie (n) the open grassland in the middle of North America.

puff of smoke (n) a small cloud of smoke.

roar (v) when a wild animal roars, it makes a loud noise to frighten other animals.

scarecrow (n) a figure of a person that farmers use to stop birds eating seeds in the fields.

screen (n) something that is used to separate different parts of a room, to hide something or to keep something private.

shy (adj) if you are shy, you don't feel confident and you are easily embarrassed.

slave (n) a person who belongs to someone else and has to work for them, but isn't paid.

smash (v) to break something into small pieces.

spear (n) a long pole with a sharp end that you use to fight or to hunt animals.

spell (n) words that make something magic happen.

stuck (adj) when something or someone is stuck, they can't move.

throne (n) a special chair for an important person like a king or queen.

tap (v) to touch something gently, making a little noise.

tin (n) a kind of metal, often used to make food cans.

tornado (n) a dangerous type of storm where the wind blows in a spiral.

turn (n) the time when someone in a group is allowed to do something.

yawn (v) when you yawn, you open your mouth very wide because you're tired or bored.

Answers

What are they? What can they do?

1. B, c
2. E, a
3. D, b
4. A, e
5. C, d

Missing words

1. heart
2. home
3. city
4. tricks
5. water
6. coward

Mixed-up story

I, G, F, C, E, B, H, D, A

I want...

The lion - A
The tin man - B
The scarecrow - A
Dorothy - A

Who's who?

1. B
2. C
3. A
4. E
5. D
6. F

You can find information about other Usborne English Readers here: www.usborneenglishreaders.com

Designed by Jodie Smith

Series designer: Laura Nelson

Edited by Jane Chisholm

With thanks to Rosie Hore

Page 40: photo of L. Frank Baum © The Granger Collection/Topfoto
Page 46: picture of hot air balloon © AVA Bitter/Shutterstock

First published in 2016 by Usborne Publishing Ltd.,
Usborne House, 83-85 Saffron Hill, London EC1N 8RT, England.
www.usborne.com